Mi gato, Mi perro

My Cat, My Dog

By Katrina Streza
Illustrated by Brenda Ponnay

xist Publishing

Mi gato es un buen gato.

My cat is a
good cat.

Mi perro es un buen perro.

My dog is a
good dog.

4

Mi gato piensa
que mi perro no
es un buen perro.

My cat thinks
my dog is
not a good dog.

Mi gato puede jugar.

My cat can play.

Mi perro puede jugar.

My dog can play.

Mi gato no juega con mi perro.

Rrrrrrow!

Rrrrrow!

My cat will not play
with my dog.

Mi gato puede correr.

My cat can run.

Mi perro puede correr.

My dog can run.

12

Mi gato puede correr
y huir de mi perro.

My cat can run away
from my dog.

Mi gato es gracioso.

My cat is funny.

Mi perro es gracioso.

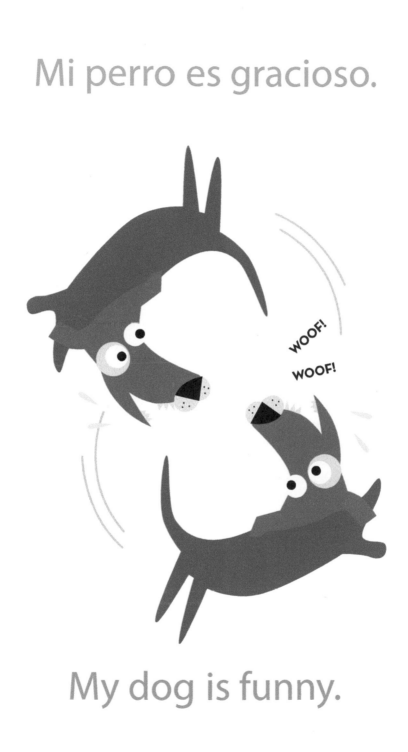

My dog is funny.

Mi gato piensa que mi perro no es gracioso.

My cat thinks
my dog is not funny.

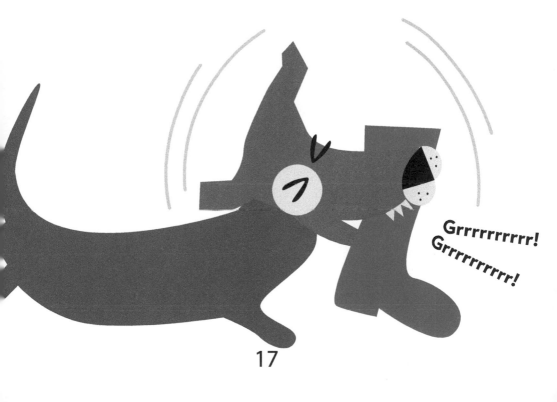

Mi gato puede saltar.

My cat can jump.

Mi perro puede saltar.

My dog can jump.

Mi gato puede saltar
aquí arriba.

My cat can
jump up here.

Mi gato puede
meterse a la caja.

My cat can
go in the box.

Mi perro puede
meterse a la caja.

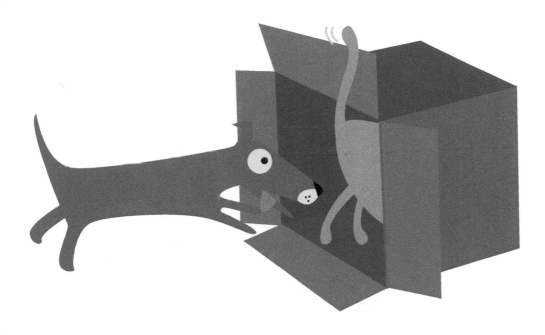

My dog can
go in the box.

Mi gato no se
meterá a la caja
con mi perro.

My cat will
not go in the box
with my dog.

Mi gato puede dormir.

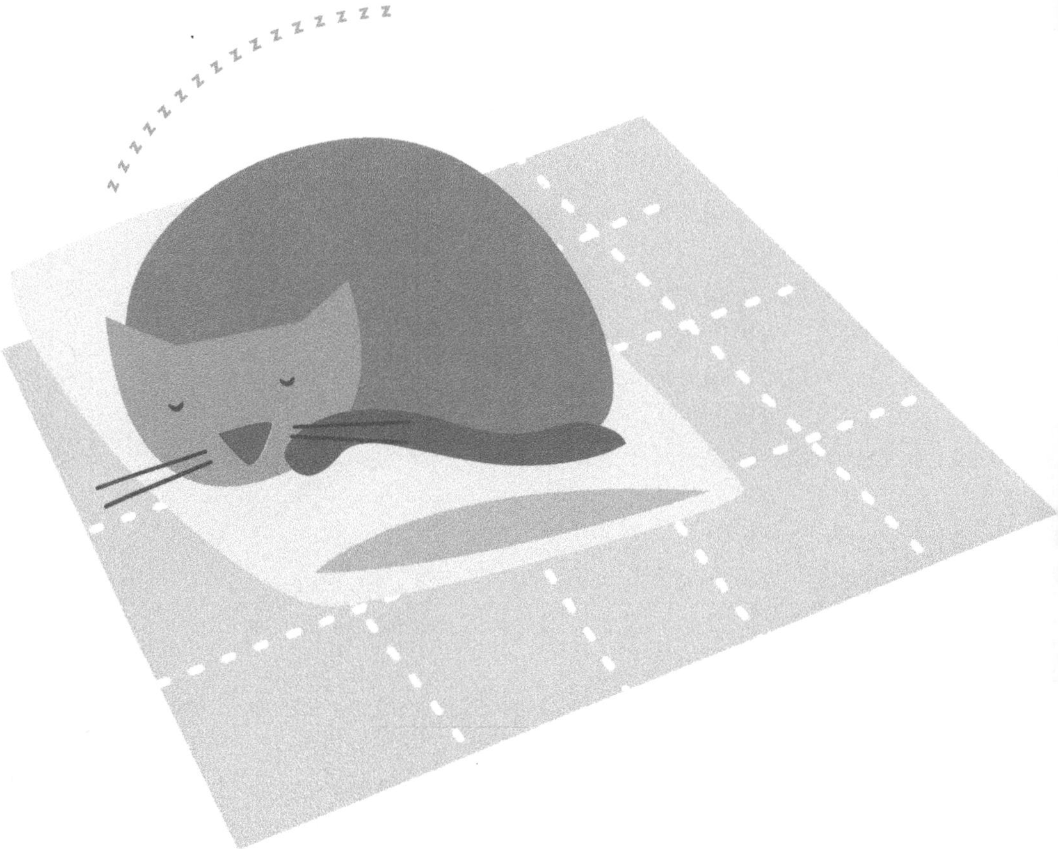
zzzzzzzzzzzzzzzzzz

My cat can sleep.

Mi perro puede dormir.

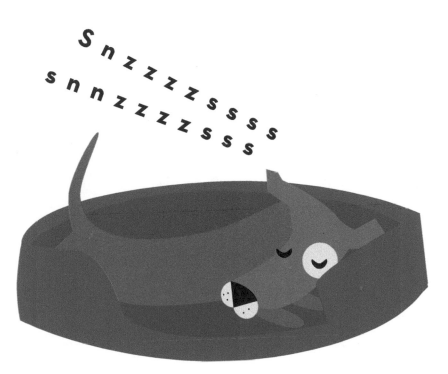

Snzzzzsss
snnzzzzsss

My dog can sleep.

Snzzzzssss
snnzzzzsss

Mi gato puede
dormir encima de
mi perro.

My cat can
sleep on my dog.

About the Author

Katrina Streza lives on a small ranch in Southern California with her family, twelve chickens, two cats, two dogs, one horse, one baby goat and one very noisy dove.

While receiving her Master's Degree in Education at Pepperdine University, Katrina decided that her goal was to make class so fun her students wouldn't realize they were learning. She's applied that philosophy while teaching and tutoring kids from kindergarten to college.

About the Illustrator

Brenda Ponnay is the author and illustrator of several children's books including the Time for Bunny series and Secret Agent Josephine series. She lives in Southern California with her daughter, Bug* who inspires her daily.

You can read all about their crazy adventures on her personal blog: www.secret-agent-josephine.com

*Not her real name.